STAR WARS
KNIGHT ERRANT
AFLAME

VOLUME ONE

SCRIPT
JOHN JACKSON MILLER

ART
FEDERICO DALLOCCHIO

COLORS
MICHAEL ATIYEH

LETTERING
MICHAEL HEISLER

COVER ART
JOE QUINONES

It is a dark age for the Republic. A thousand years before Obi-Wan Kenobi met Anakin Skywalker, their Jedi forebears struggle in vain against a rampaging Sith menace. The Republic abandons vast swaths of territory, deactivating many of the communications relays that once bound the galaxy.

But the Sith have other enemies—themselves. Sith Lords battle each other for the right to finish off the Republic. Far behind Sith lines, on Chelloa, Lord Daiman makes a discovery he hopes will help him rise above the other petty princelings once and for all. The Republic is in peril.

Learning of the danger, the charismatic Jedi Master Vannar Treece leads a group of volunteers on what many expect will be a one-way mission. Treece, a veteran campaigner, is more confident. But he cannot plan for everything—and, alone in Sith space, that is usually fatal . . .

This story takes place approximately 1,032 years BBY.

DARK HORSE COMICS

Spotlight

visit us at www.abdopublishing.com

Reinforced library bound edition published in 2012 by Spotlight,
a division of the ABDO Group, PO Box 398166, Minneapolis, MN 55439.
Spotlight produces high-quality reinforced library bound editions for schools and libraries.
Published by agreement with Dark Horse Comics, Inc., and Lucasfilm Ltd.

Printed in the United States of America, North Mankato, Minnesota.
102011
012012
♲ This book contains at least 10% recycled materials.

Library of Congress Cataloging-in-Publication Data

Miller, John Jackson.
  Star wars : knight errant. volume 1 Aflame / script, John Jackson Miller ; pencils, Federico
Dallocchio. -- Reinforced library bound ed.
    p. cm.
  "Dark Horse."
  "LucasFilm."
  Summary: Eighteen-year-old Kerra Holt, a Jedi Knight on her first mission, is left deep in
Sith space without any support or resources and realizes how unprepared she is, but will not
abandon the Jedi's mission to help the colony.
  ISBN 978-1-59961-986-6 (volume 1) -- ISBN 978-1-59961-987-3 (volume 2)
  ISBN 978-1-59961-988-0 (volume 3) -- ISBN 978-1-59961-989-7 (volume 4)
  ISBN 978-1-59961-990-3 (volume 5)
  1. Graphic novels. [1. Graphic novels. 2. Science fiction.] I. Dallocchio, Federico, ill. II. Title.
III. Title: Knight errant. IV. Title: Aflame.
  PZ7.7.M535St 2012
  741.5'973--dc23

                                        2011031240

All Spotlight books are reinforced library binding
and manufactured in the United States of America.

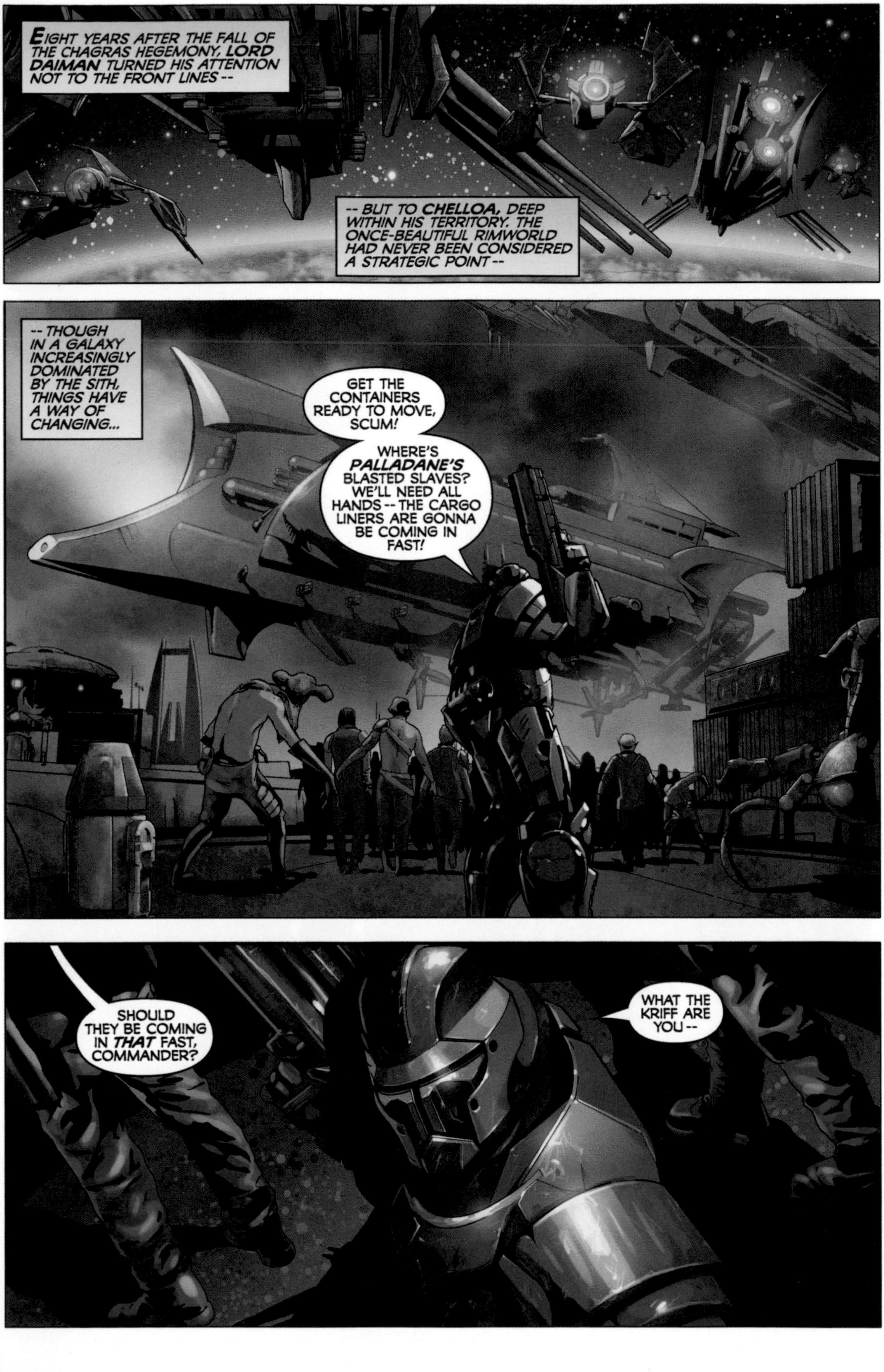
EIGHT YEARS AFTER THE FALL OF THE CHAGRAS HEGEMONY, LORD DAIMAN TURNED HIS ATTENTION NOT TO THE FRONT LINES --
-- BUT TO CHELLOA, DEEP WITHIN HIS TERRITORY. THE ONCE-BEAUTIFUL RIMWORLD HAD NEVER BEEN CONSIDERED A STRATEGIC POINT --
-- THOUGH IN A GALAXY INCREASINGLY DOMINATED BY THE SITH, THINGS HAVE A WAY OF CHANGING...
GET THE CONTAINERS READY TO MOVE, SCUM!
WHERE'S PALLADANE'S BLASTED SLAVES? WE'LL NEED ALL HANDS -- THE CARGO LINERS ARE GONNA BE COMING IN FAST!
SHOULD THEY BE COMING IN THAT FAST, COMMANDER?
WHAT THE KRIFF ARE YOU --

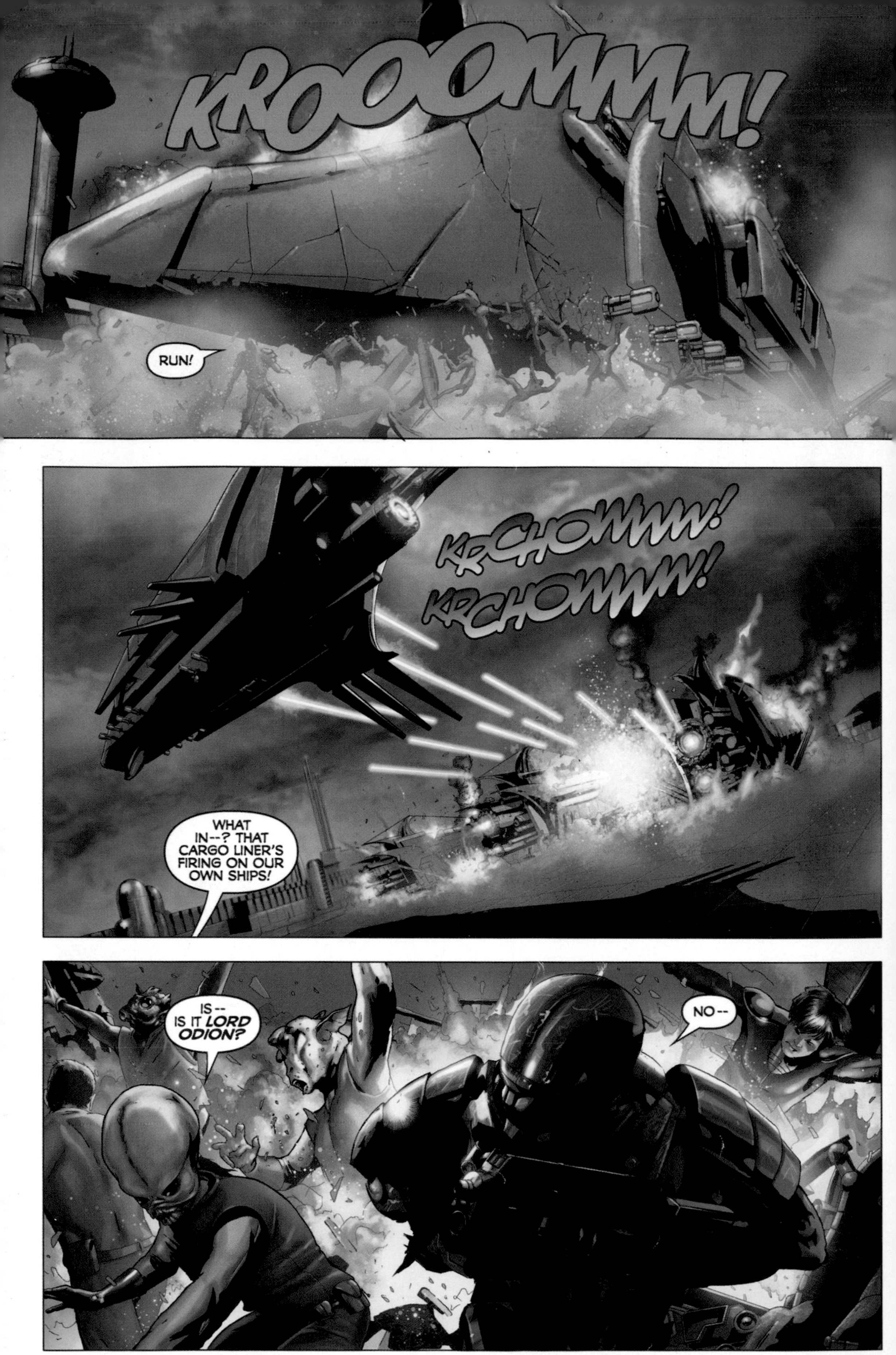
KROOOMMM!
RUN!
KRCHOWWW!
KRCHOWWW!
WHAT IN--? THAT CARGO LINER'S FIRING ON OUR OWN SHIPS!
IS -- IS IT LORD ODION?
NO--

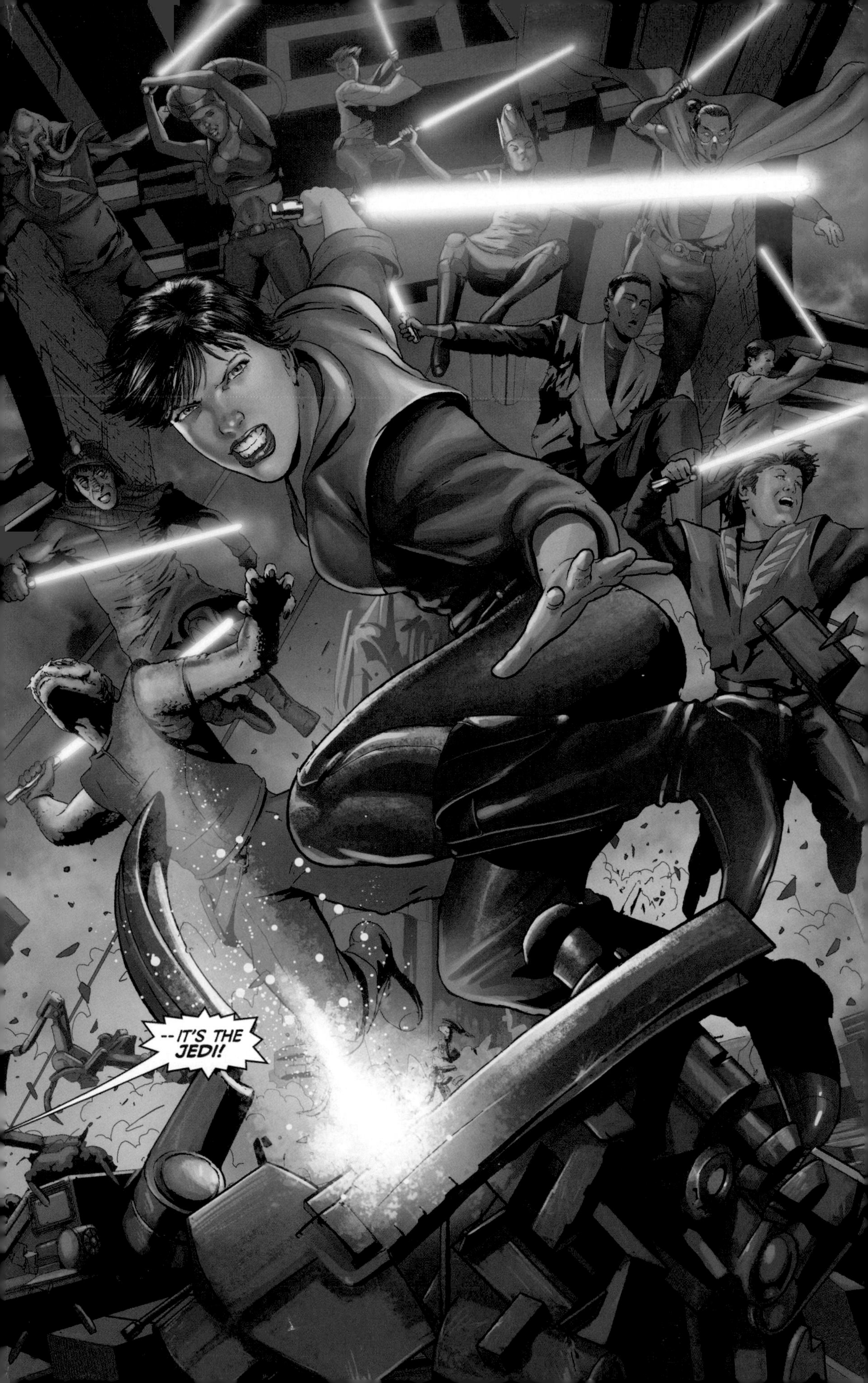
--IT'S THE JEDI!

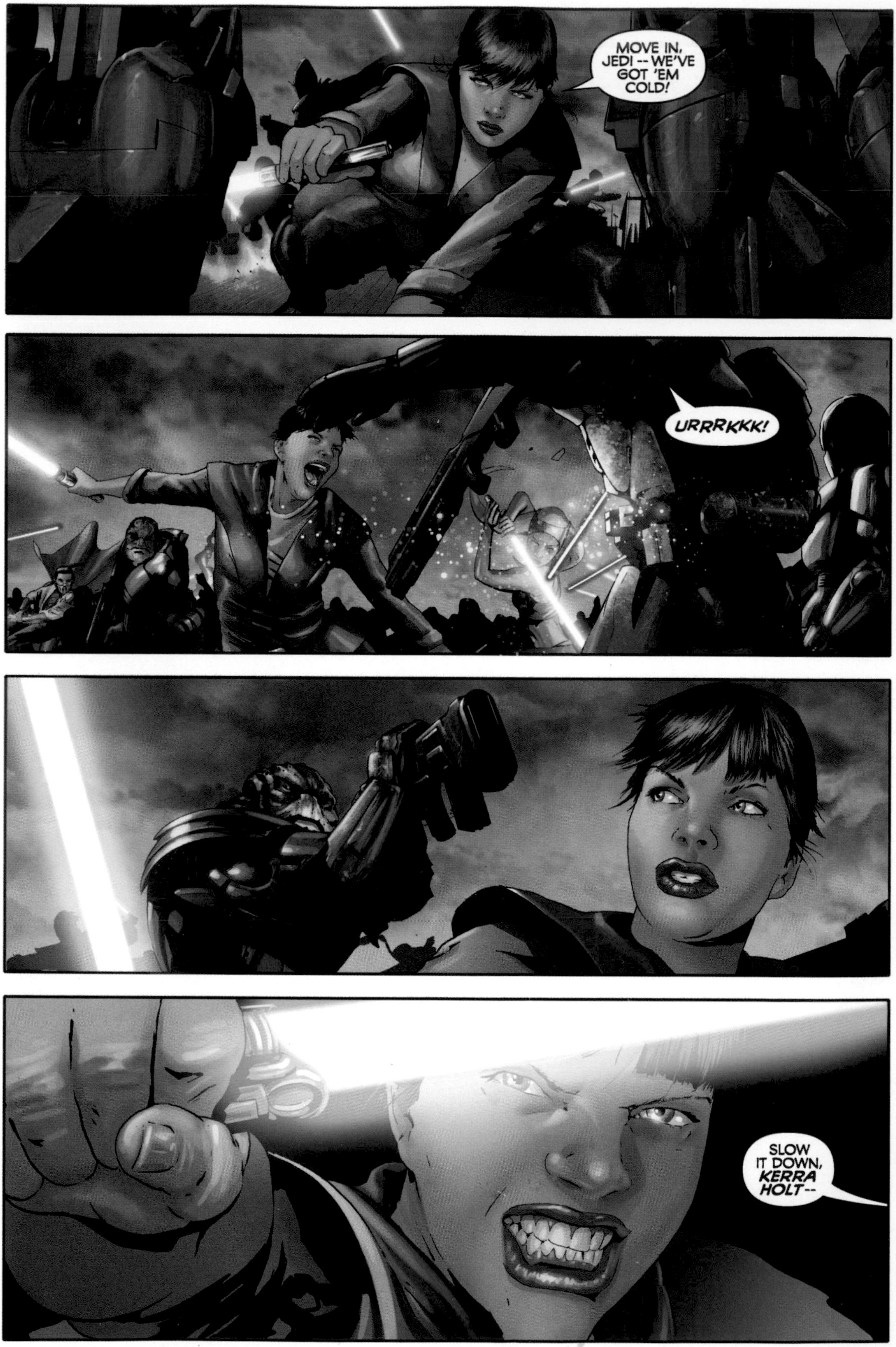
MOVE IN, JEDI -- WE'VE GOT 'EM COLD!
URRRKKK!
SLOW IT DOWN, *KERRA HOLT*--

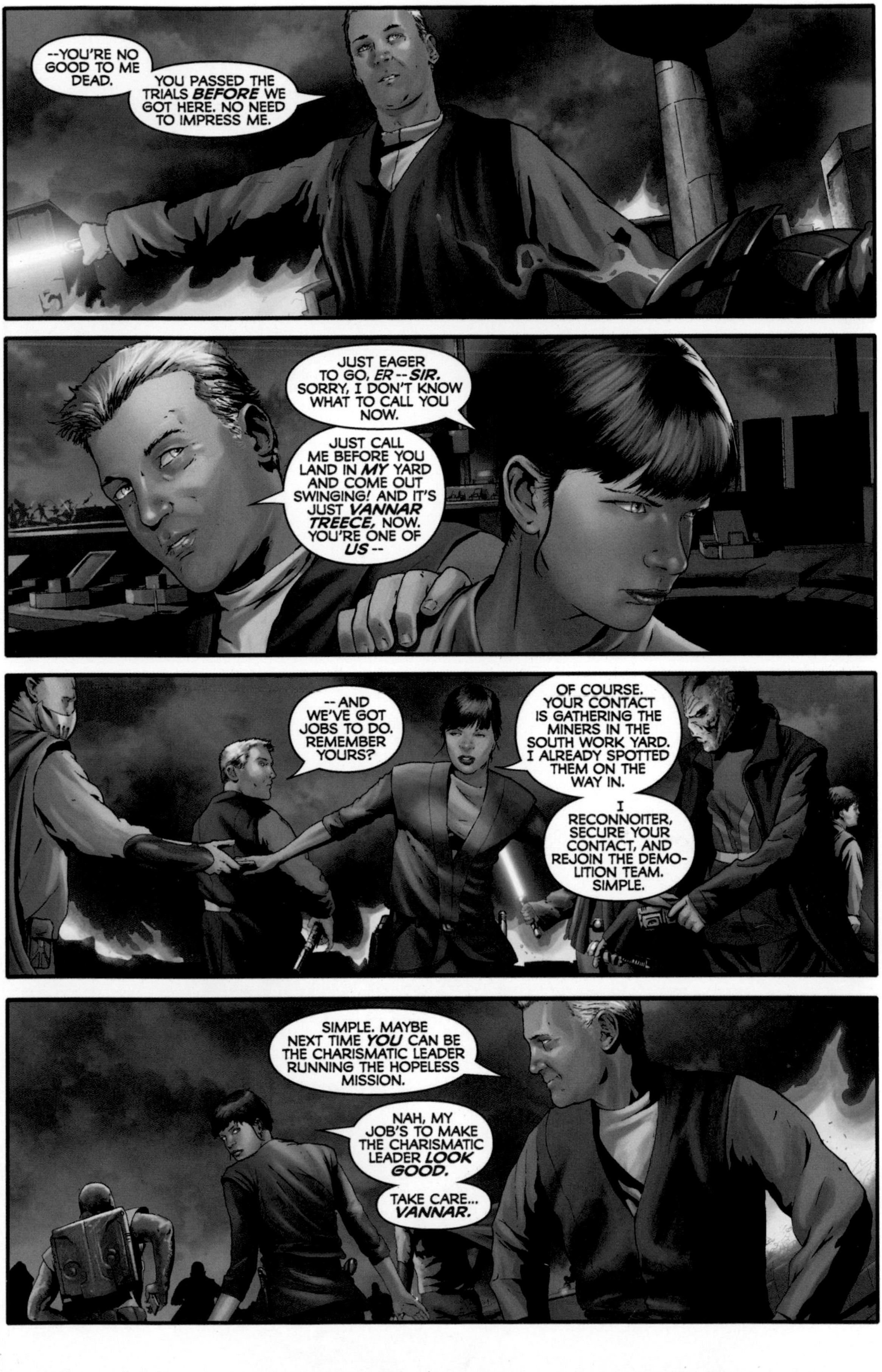
--YOU'RE NO GOOD TO ME DEAD.
YOU PASSED THE TRIALS BEFORE WE GOT HERE. NO NEED TO IMPRESS ME.
JUST EAGER TO GO, ER--SIR. SORRY, I DON'T KNOW WHAT TO CALL YOU NOW.
JUST CALL ME BEFORE YOU LAND IN MY YARD AND COME OUT SWINGING! AND IT'S JUST VANNAR TREECE, NOW. YOU'RE ONE OF US--
--AND WE'VE GOT JOBS TO DO. REMEMBER YOURS?
OF COURSE. YOUR CONTACT IS GATHERING THE MINERS IN THE SOUTH WORK YARD. I ALREADY SPOTTED THEM ON THE WAY IN.
I RECONNOITER, SECURE YOUR CONTACT, AND REJOIN THE DEMOLITION TEAM. SIMPLE.
SIMPLE. MAYBE NEXT TIME YOU CAN BE THE CHARISMATIC LEADER RUNNING THE HOPELESS MISSION.
NAH, MY JOB'S TO MAKE THE CHARISMATIC LEADER LOOK GOOD.
TAKE CARE... VANNAR.

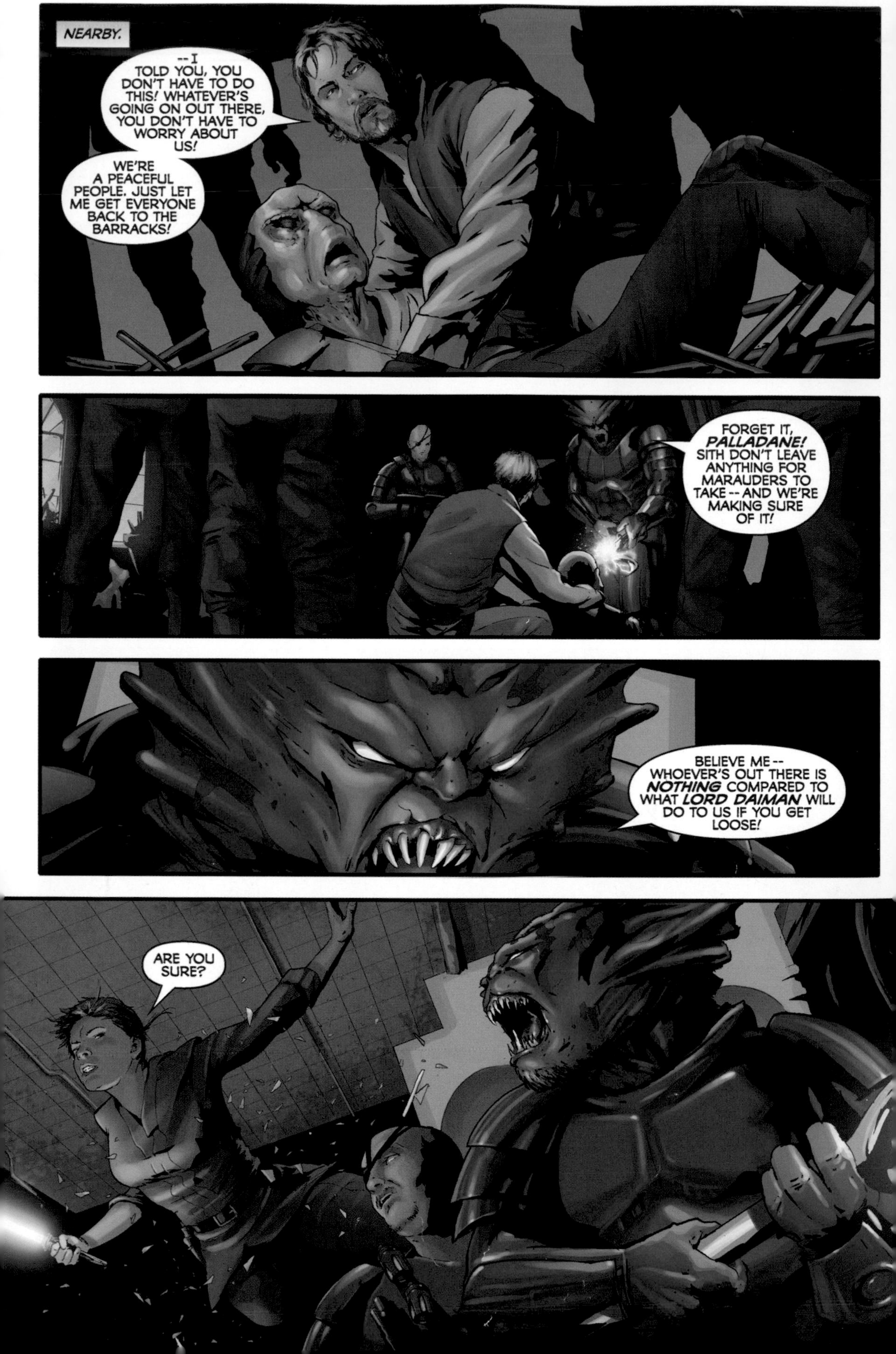

NEARBY.
--I TOLD YOU, YOU DON'T HAVE TO DO THIS! WHATEVER'S GOING ON OUT THERE, YOU DON'T HAVE TO WORRY ABOUT US!
WE'RE A PEACEFUL PEOPLE. JUST LET ME GET EVERYONE BACK TO THE BARRACKS!
FORGET IT, *PALLADANE!* SITH DON'T LEAVE ANYTHING FOR MARAUDERS TO TAKE -- AND WE'RE MAKING SURE OF IT!
BELIEVE ME -- WHOEVER'S OUT THERE IS *NOTHING* COMPARED TO WHAT *LORD DAIMAN* WILL DO TO US IF YOU GET LOOSE!
ARE YOU SURE?

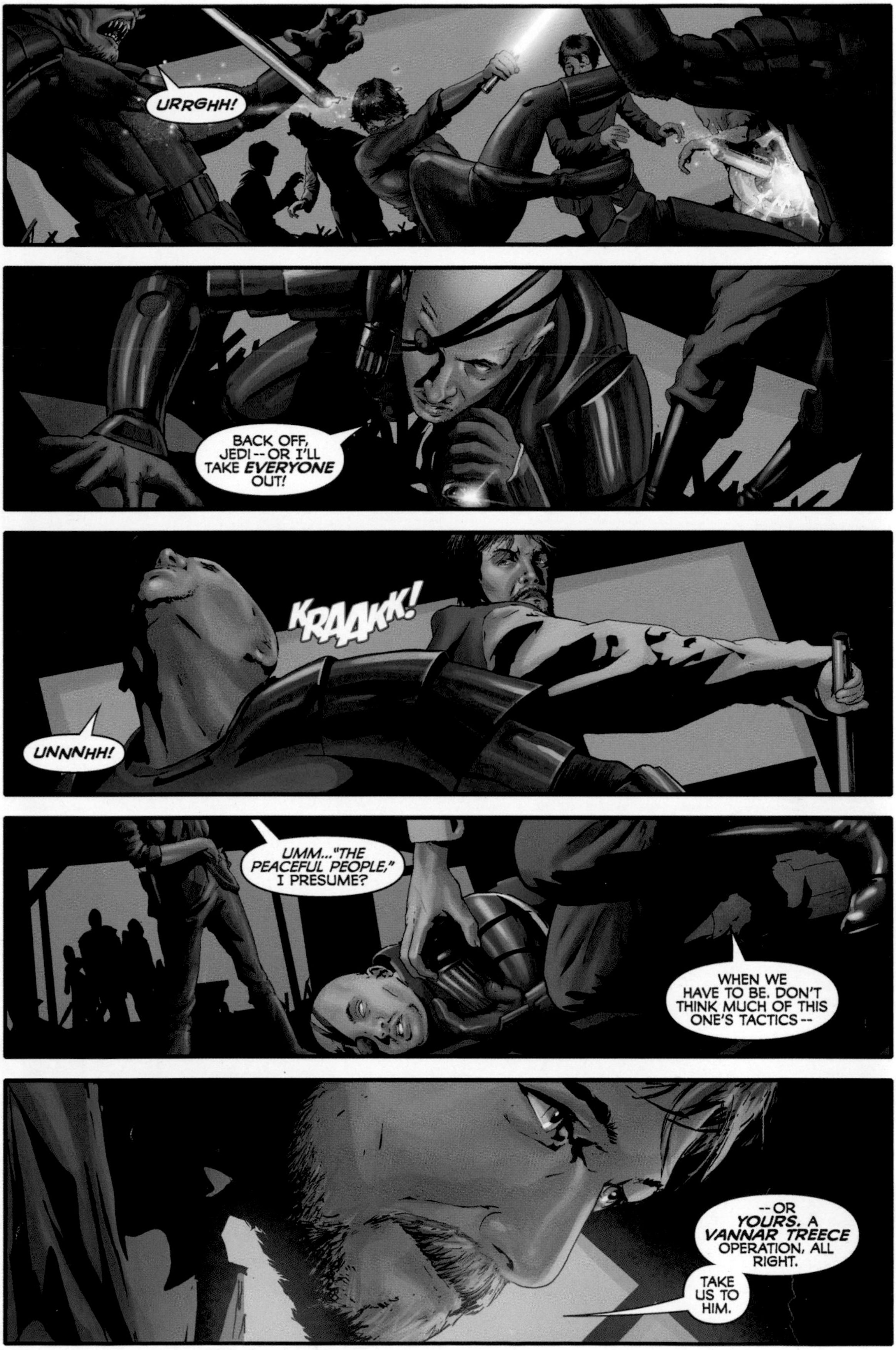
URRGHH!
BACK OFF, JEDI--OR I'LL TAKE *EVERYONE* OUT!
KRAAKK!
UNNNHH!
UMM..."THE PEACEFUL PEOPLE," I PRESUME?
WHEN WE HAVE TO BE. DON'T THINK MUCH OF THIS ONE'S TACTICS--
--OR *YOURS.* A *VANNAR TREECE* OPERATION, ALL RIGHT.
TAKE US TO HIM.

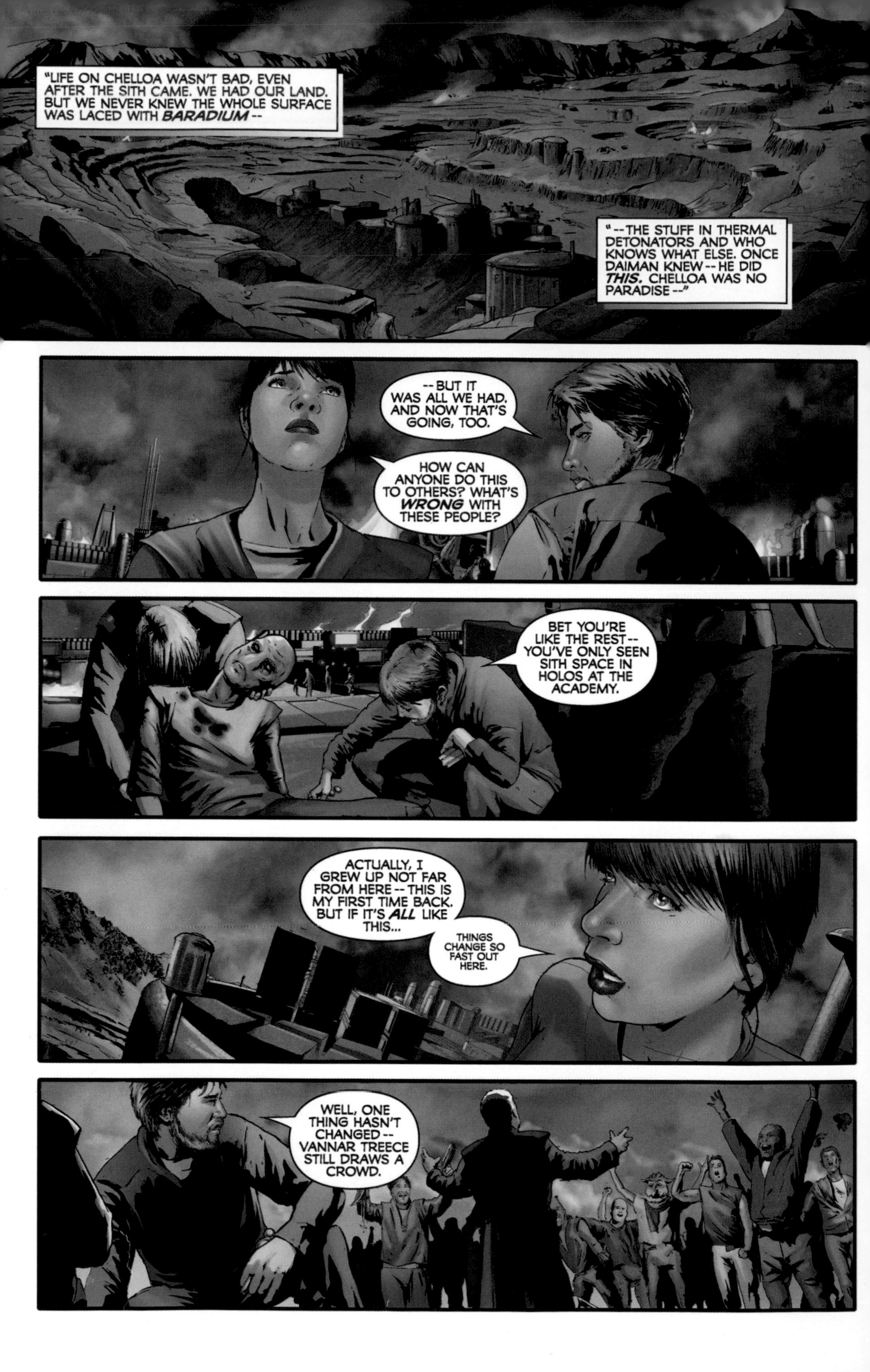
"LIFE ON CHELLOA WASN'T BAD, EVEN AFTER THE SITH CAME. WE HAD OUR LAND. BUT WE NEVER KNEW THE WHOLE SURFACE WAS LACED WITH BARADIUM --
"--THE STUFF IN THERMAL DETONATORS AND WHO KNOWS WHAT ELSE. ONCE DAIMAN KNEW -- HE DID THIS. CHELLOA WAS NO PARADISE --"
--BUT IT WAS ALL WE HAD. AND NOW THAT'S GOING, TOO.
HOW CAN ANYONE DO THIS TO OTHERS? WHAT'S WRONG WITH THESE PEOPLE?
BET YOU'RE LIKE THE REST -- YOU'VE ONLY SEEN SITH SPACE IN HOLOS AT THE ACADEMY.
ACTUALLY, I GREW UP NOT FAR FROM HERE -- THIS IS MY FIRST TIME BACK. BUT IF IT'S ALL LIKE THIS...
THINGS CHANGE SO FAST OUT HERE.
WELL, ONE THING HASN'T CHANGED -- VANNAR TREECE STILL DRAWS A CROWD.

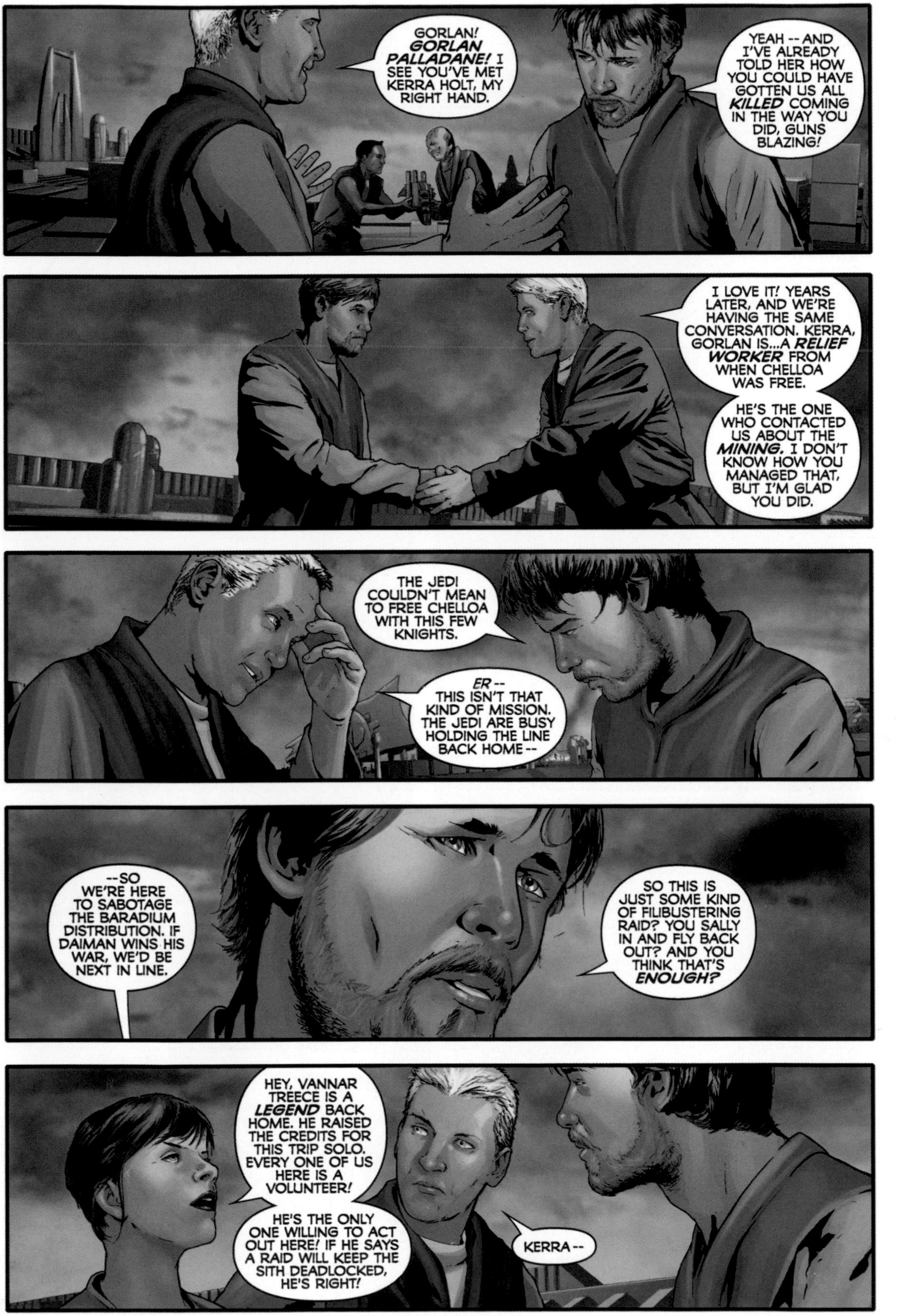
GORLAN! GORLAN PALLADANE! I SEE YOU'VE MET KERRA HOLT, MY RIGHT HAND.
YEAH -- AND I'VE ALREADY TOLD HER HOW YOU COULD HAVE GOTTEN US ALL KILLED COMING IN THE WAY YOU DID, GUNS BLAZING!
I LOVE IT! YEARS LATER, AND WE'RE HAVING THE SAME CONVERSATION. KERRA, GORLAN IS...A RELIEF WORKER FROM WHEN CHELLOA WAS FREE.
HE'S THE ONE WHO CONTACTED US ABOUT THE MINING. I DON'T KNOW HOW YOU MANAGED THAT, BUT I'M GLAD YOU DID.
THE JEDI COULDN'T MEAN TO FREE CHELLOA WITH THIS FEW KNIGHTS.
ER -- THIS ISN'T THAT KIND OF MISSION. THE JEDI ARE BUSY HOLDING THE LINE BACK HOME --
--SO WE'RE HERE TO SABOTAGE THE BARADIUM DISTRIBUTION. IF DAIMAN WINS HIS WAR, WE'D BE NEXT IN LINE.
SO THIS IS JUST SOME KIND OF FILIBUSTERING RAID? YOU SALLY IN AND FLY BACK OUT? AND YOU THINK THAT'S ENOUGH?
HEY, VANNAR TREECE IS A LEGEND BACK HOME. HE RAISED THE CREDITS FOR THIS TRIP SOLO. EVERY ONE OF US HERE IS A VOLUNTEER!
HE'S THE ONLY ONE WILLING TO ACT OUT HERE! IF HE SAYS A RAID WILL KEEP THE SITH DEADLOCKED, HE'S RIGHT!
KERRA --

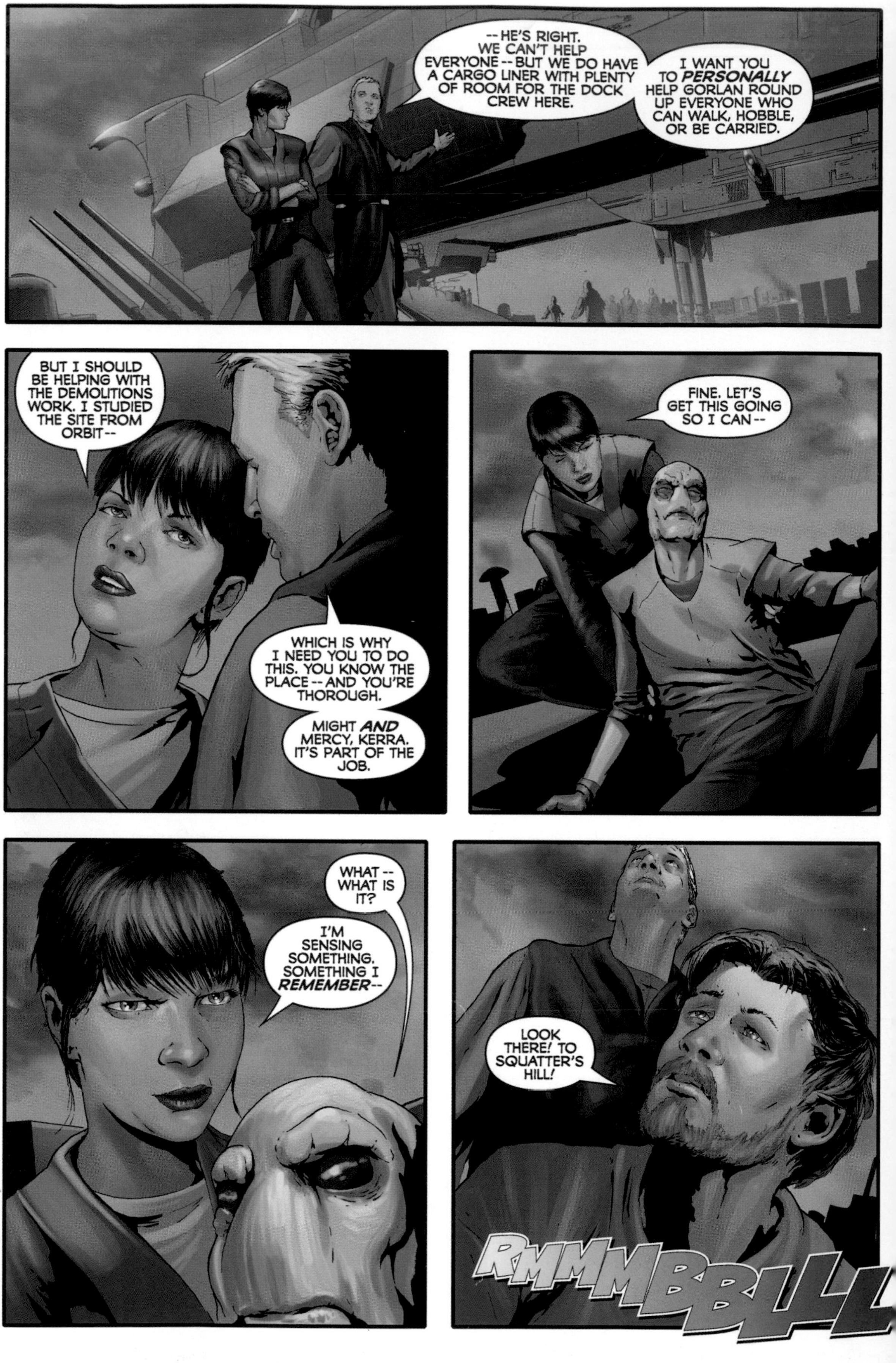
--HE'S RIGHT. WE CAN'T HELP EVERYONE--BUT WE DO HAVE A CARGO LINER WITH PLENTY OF ROOM FOR THE DOCK CREW HERE.
I WANT YOU TO *PERSONALLY* HELP GORLAN ROUND UP EVERYONE WHO CAN WALK, HOBBLE, OR BE CARRIED.
BUT I SHOULD BE HELPING WITH THE DEMOLITIONS WORK. I STUDIED THE SITE FROM ORBIT--
WHICH IS WHY I NEED YOU TO DO THIS. YOU KNOW THE PLACE--AND YOU'RE THOROUGH.
MIGHT ***AND*** MERCY, KERRA. IT'S PART OF THE JOB.
FINE. LET'S GET THIS GOING SO I CAN--
WHAT--WHAT IS IT?
I'M SENSING SOMETHING. SOMETHING I *REMEMBER*--
LOOK THERE! TO SQUATTER'S HILL!
RMMMBBLLL

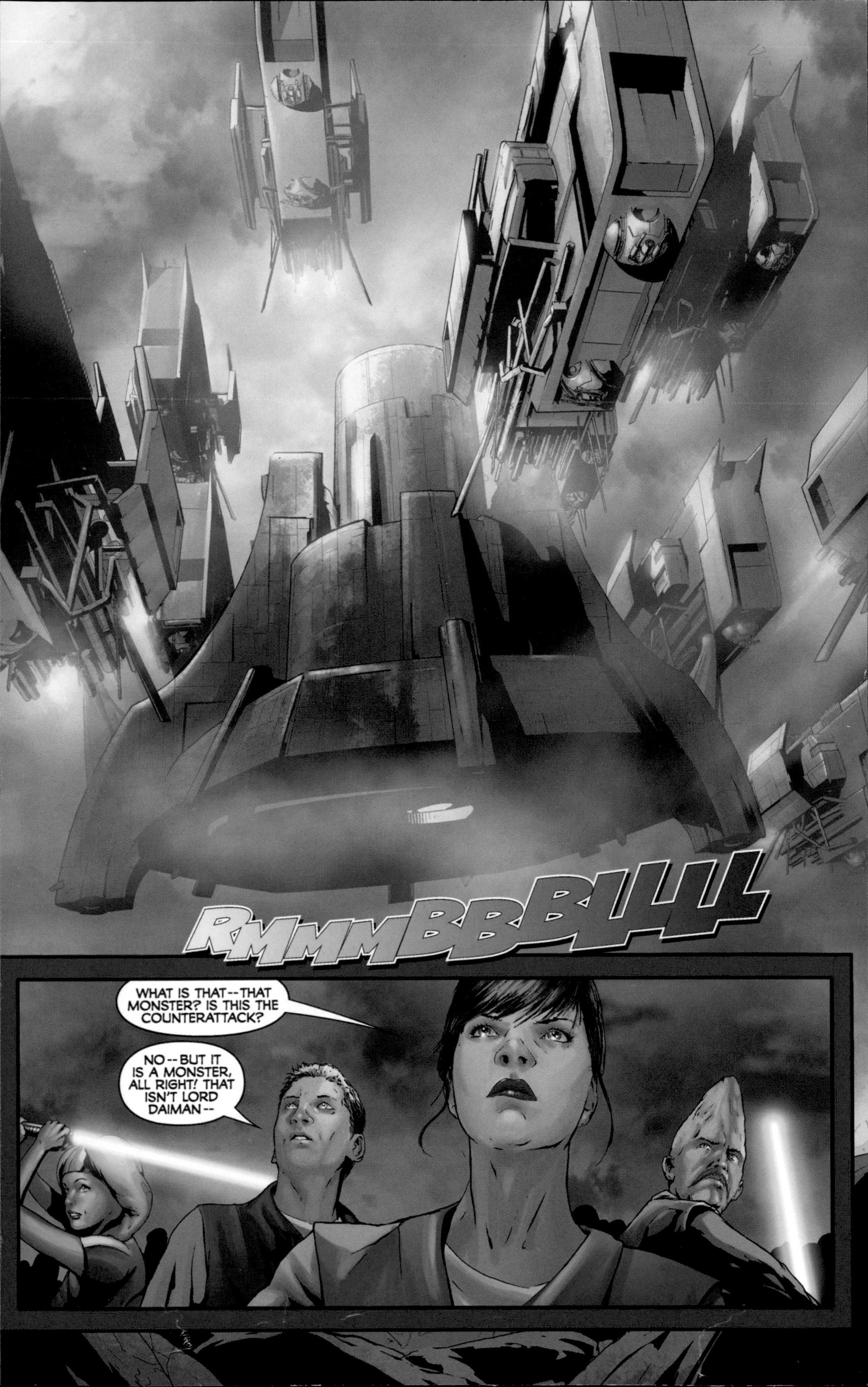
RMMMBBBLLLL
WHAT IS THAT--THAT MONSTER? IS THIS THE COUNTERATTACK?
NO--BUT IT IS A MONSTER, ALL RIGHT! THAT ISN'T LORD DAIMAN--

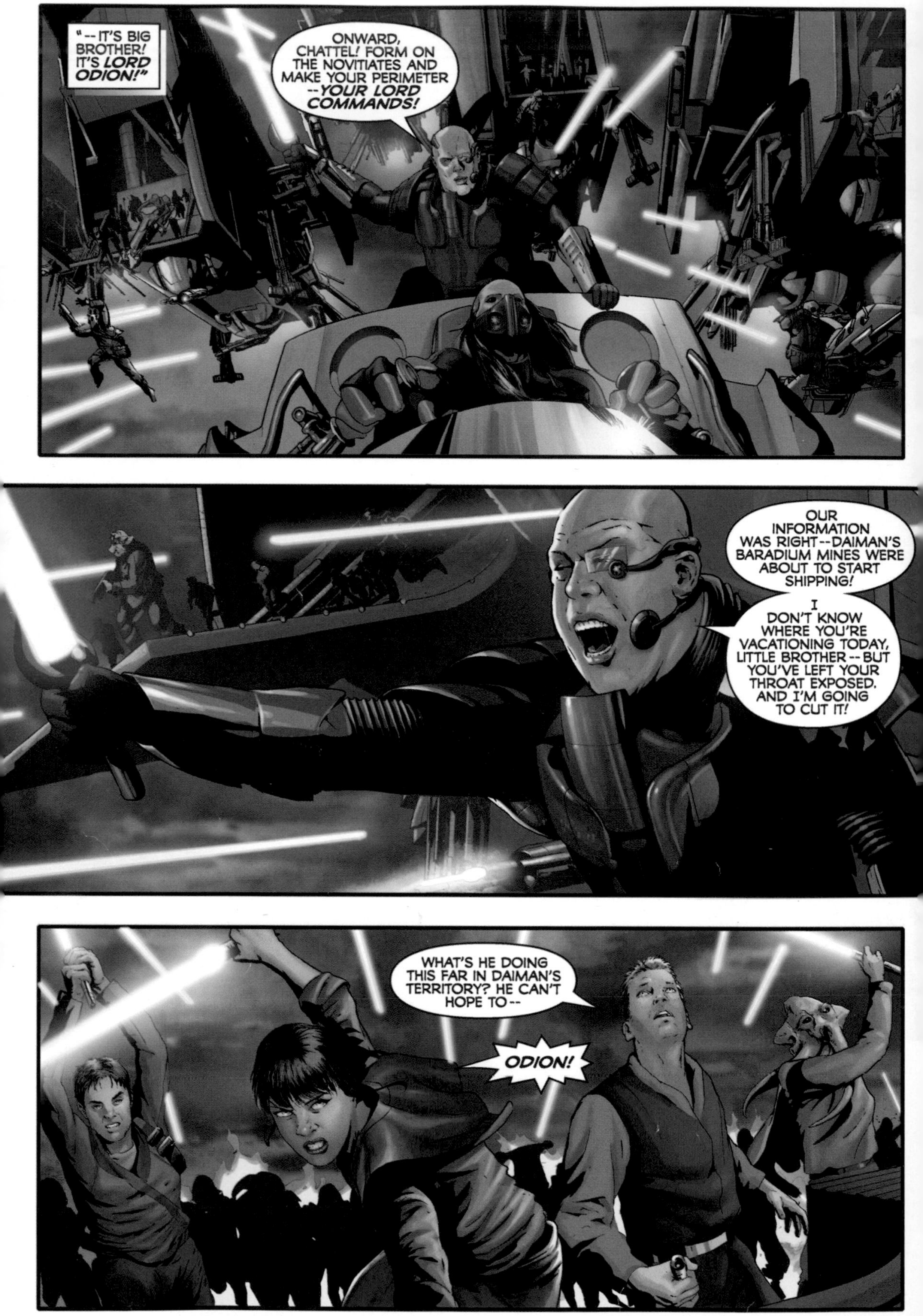
"--IT'S BIG BROTHER! IT'S *LORD ODION!*"
ONWARD, CHATTEL! FORM ON THE NOVITIATES AND MAKE YOUR PERIMETER --*YOUR LORD COMMANDS!*
OUR INFORMATION WAS RIGHT--DAIMAN'S BARADIUM MINES WERE ABOUT TO START SHIPPING!
I DON'T KNOW WHERE YOU'RE VACATIONING TODAY, LITTLE BROTHER--BUT YOU'VE LEFT YOUR THROAT EXPOSED. AND I'M GOING TO CUT IT!
WHAT'S HE DOING THIS FAR IN DAIMAN'S TERRITORY? HE CAN'T HOPE TO--
ODION!

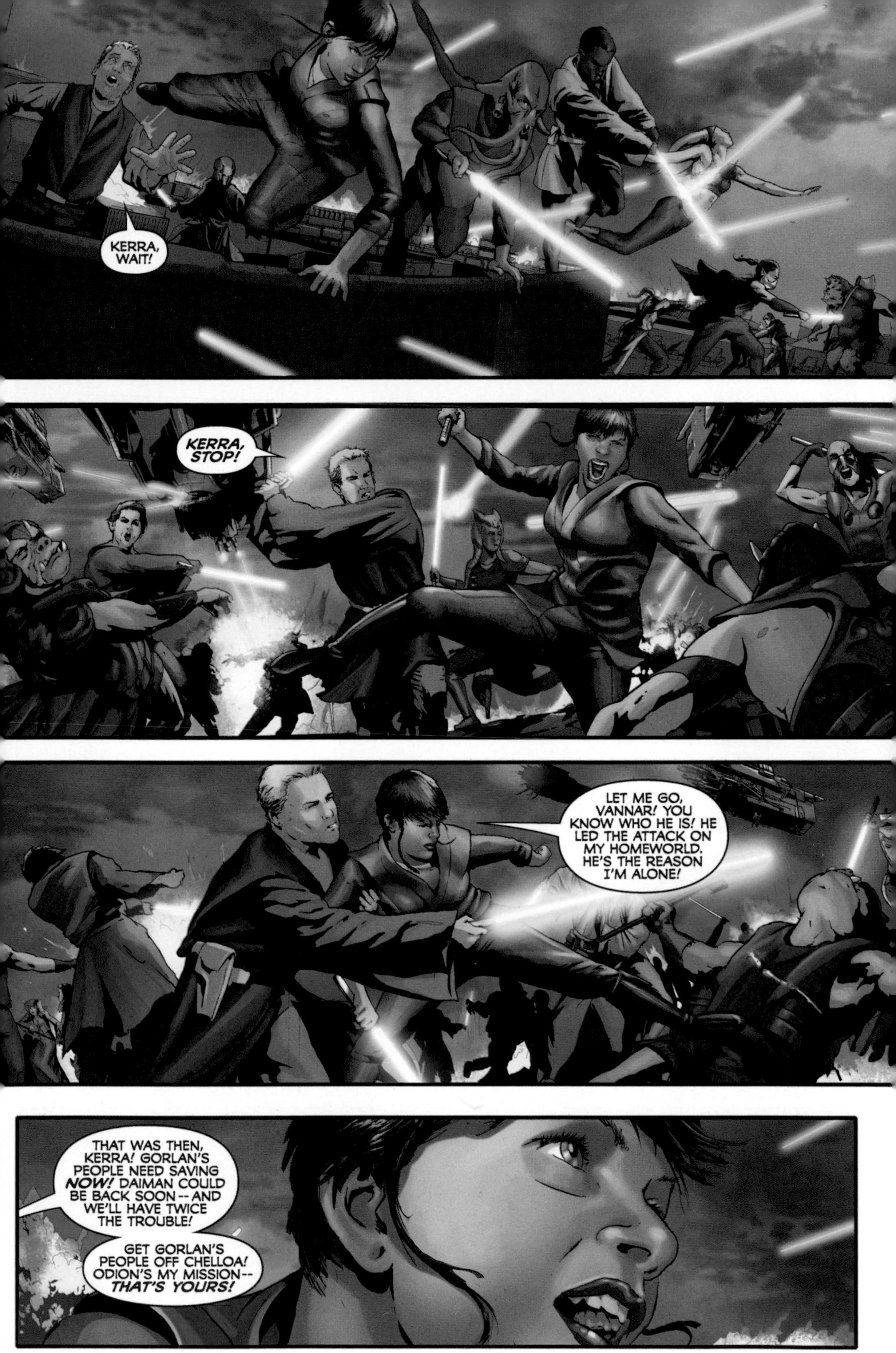
KERRA, WAIT!
KERRA, STOP!
LET ME GO, VANNAR! YOU KNOW WHO HE IS! HE LED THE ATTACK ON MY HOMEWORLD. HE'S THE REASON I'M ALONE!
THAT WAS THEN, KERRA! GORLAN'S PEOPLE NEED SAVING NOW! DAIMAN COULD BE BACK SOON--AND WE'LL HAVE TWICE THE TROUBLE!
GET GORLAN'S PEOPLE OFF CHELLOA! ODION'S MY MISSION--THAT'S YOURS!

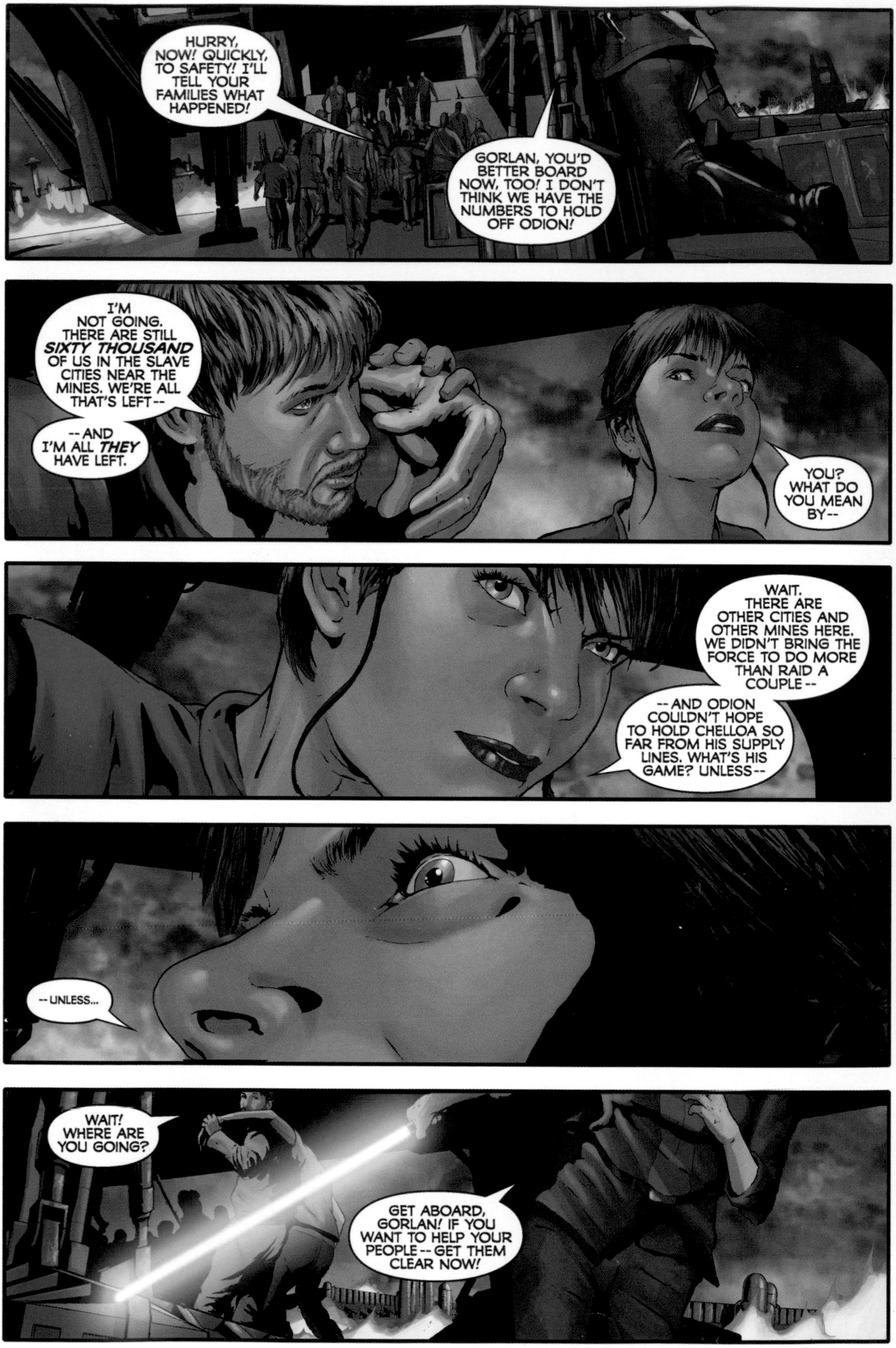
HURRY, NOW! QUICKLY, TO SAFETY! I'LL TELL YOUR FAMILIES WHAT HAPPENED!
GORLAN, YOU'D BETTER BOARD NOW, TOO! I DON'T THINK WE HAVE THE NUMBERS TO HOLD OFF ODION!
I'M NOT GOING. THERE ARE STILL SIXTY THOUSAND OF US IN THE SLAVE CITIES NEAR THE MINES. WE'RE ALL THAT'S LEFT--
--AND I'M ALL THEY HAVE LEFT.
YOU? WHAT DO YOU MEAN BY--
WAIT. THERE ARE OTHER CITIES AND OTHER MINES HERE. WE DIDN'T BRING THE FORCE TO DO MORE THAN RAID A COUPLE--
--AND ODION COULDN'T HOPE TO HOLD CHELLOA SO FAR FROM HIS SUPPLY LINES. WHAT'S HIS GAME? UNLESS--
--UNLESS...
WAIT! WHERE ARE YOU GOING?
GET ABOARD, GORLAN! IF YOU WANT TO HELP YOUR PEOPLE--GET THEM CLEAR NOW!

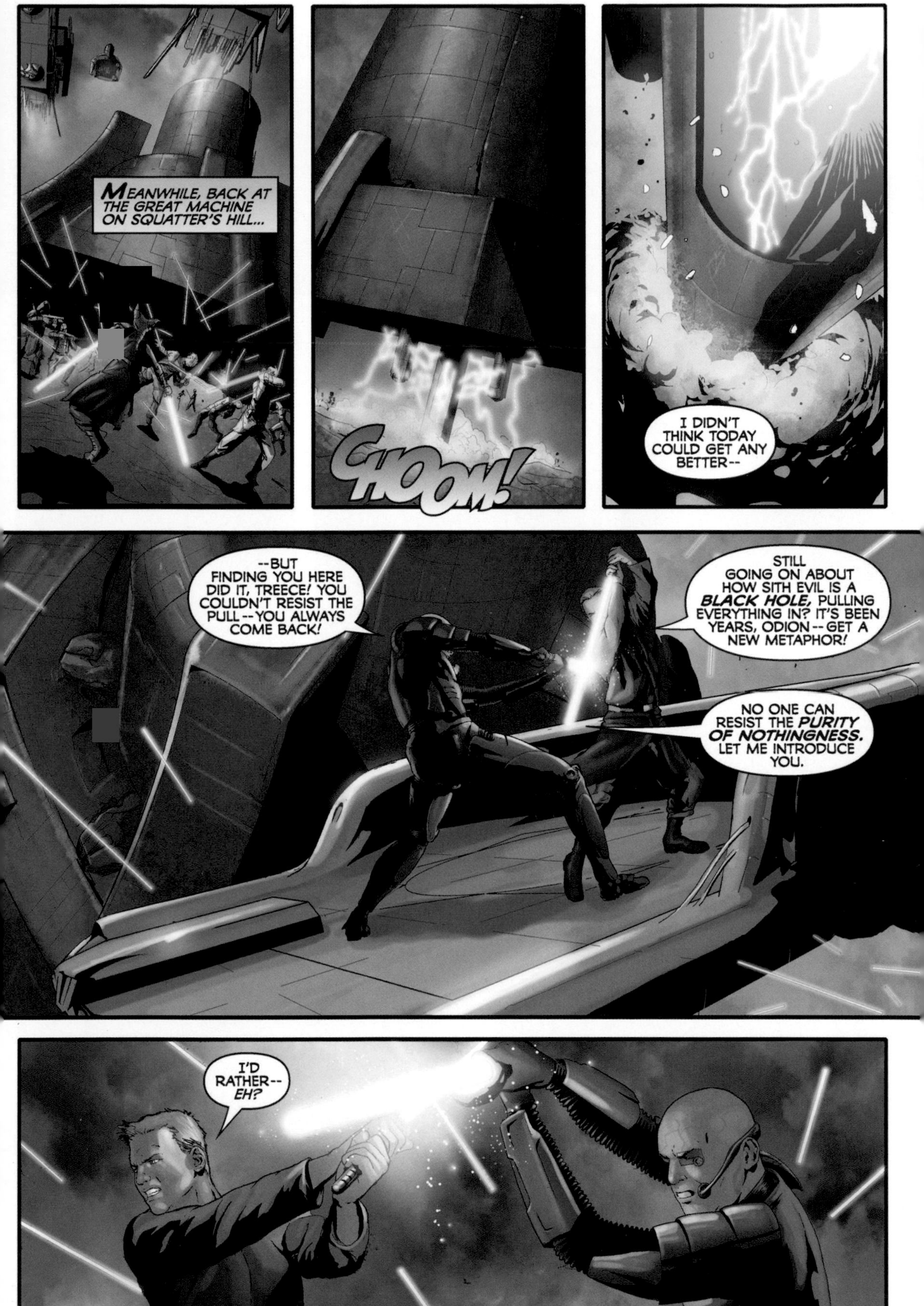
MEANWHILE, BACK AT THE GREAT MACHINE ON SQUATTER'S HILL...
CHOOM!
I DIDN'T THINK TODAY COULD GET ANY BETTER--
--BUT FINDING YOU HERE DID IT, TREECE! YOU COULDN'T RESIST THE PULL--YOU ALWAYS COME BACK!
STILL GOING ON ABOUT HOW SITH EVIL IS A BLACK HOLE, PULLING EVERYTHING IN? IT'S BEEN YEARS, ODION--GET A NEW METAPHOR!
NO ONE CAN RESIST THE PURITY OF NOTHINGNESS. LET ME INTRODUCE YOU.
I'D RATHER-- EH?

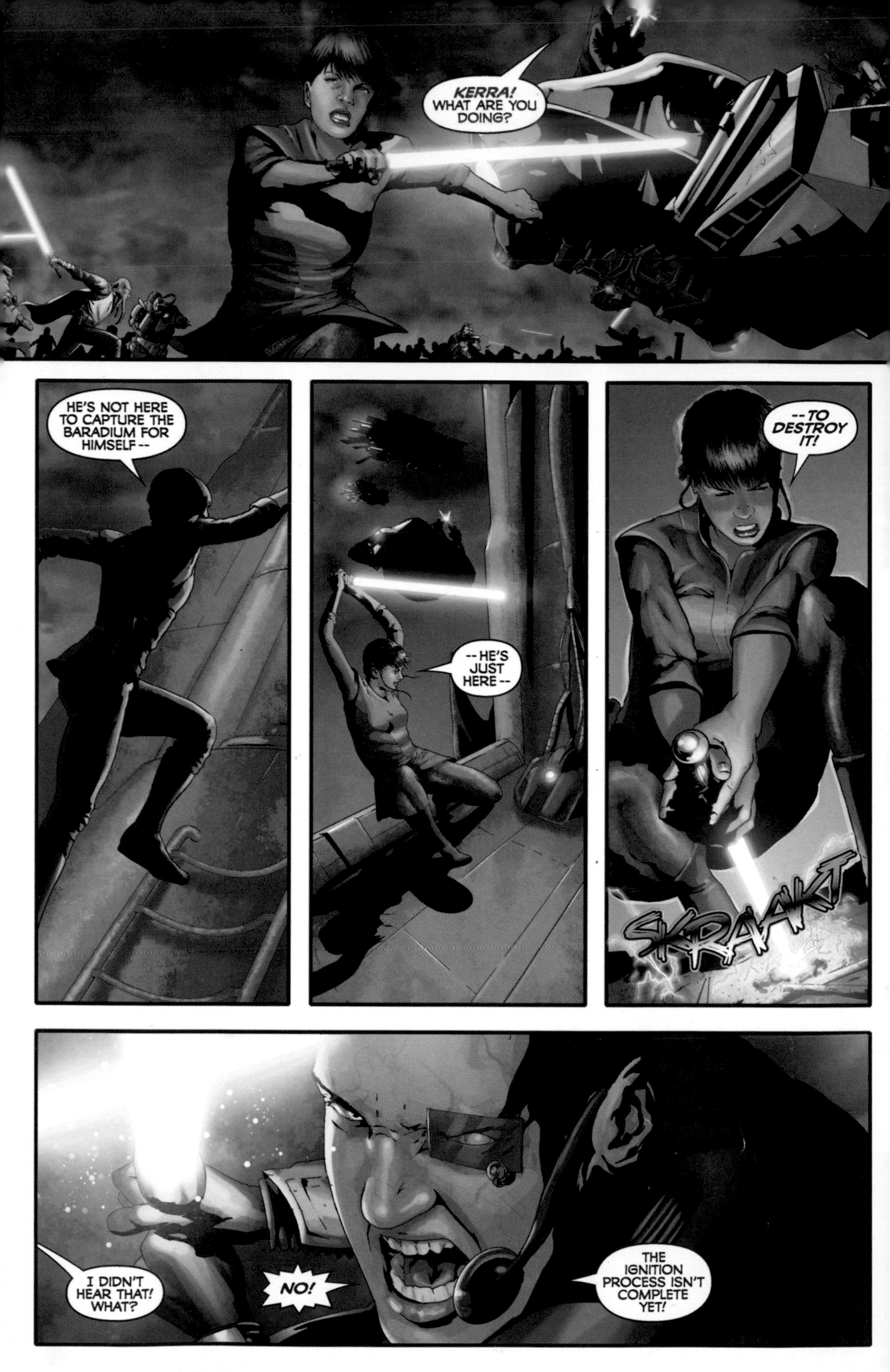
KERRA! WHAT ARE YOU DOING?
HE'S NOT HERE TO CAPTURE THE BARADIUM FOR HIMSELF --
-- HE'S JUST HERE --
-- TO DESTROY IT!
SKRAAKT
I DIDN'T HEAR THAT! WHAT?
NO!
THE IGNITION PROCESS ISN'T COMPLETE YET!

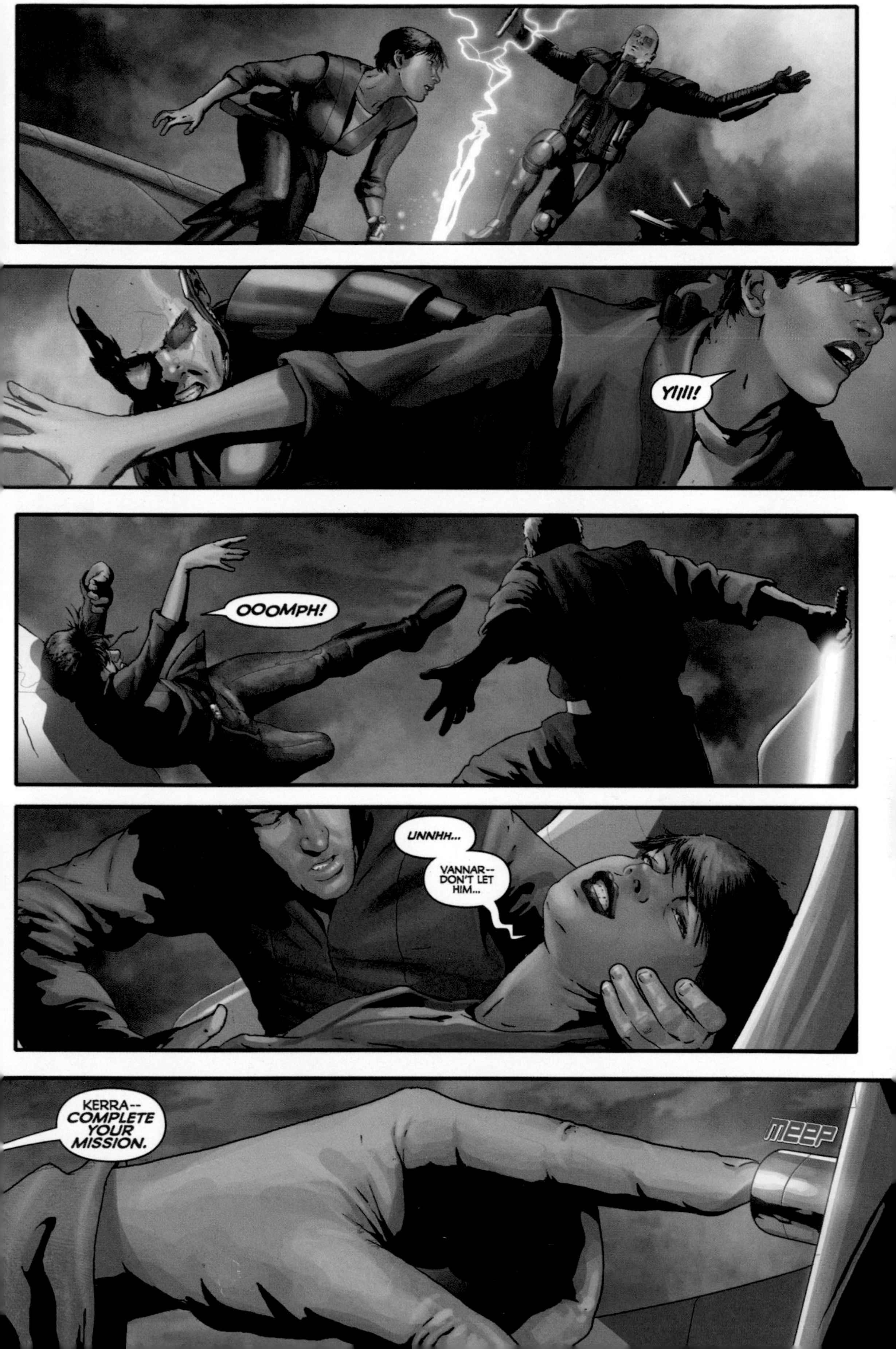

YIIII!
OOOMPH!
UNNHH...
VANNAR-- DON'T LET HIM...
KERRA-- COMPLETE YOUR MISSION.
MEEP

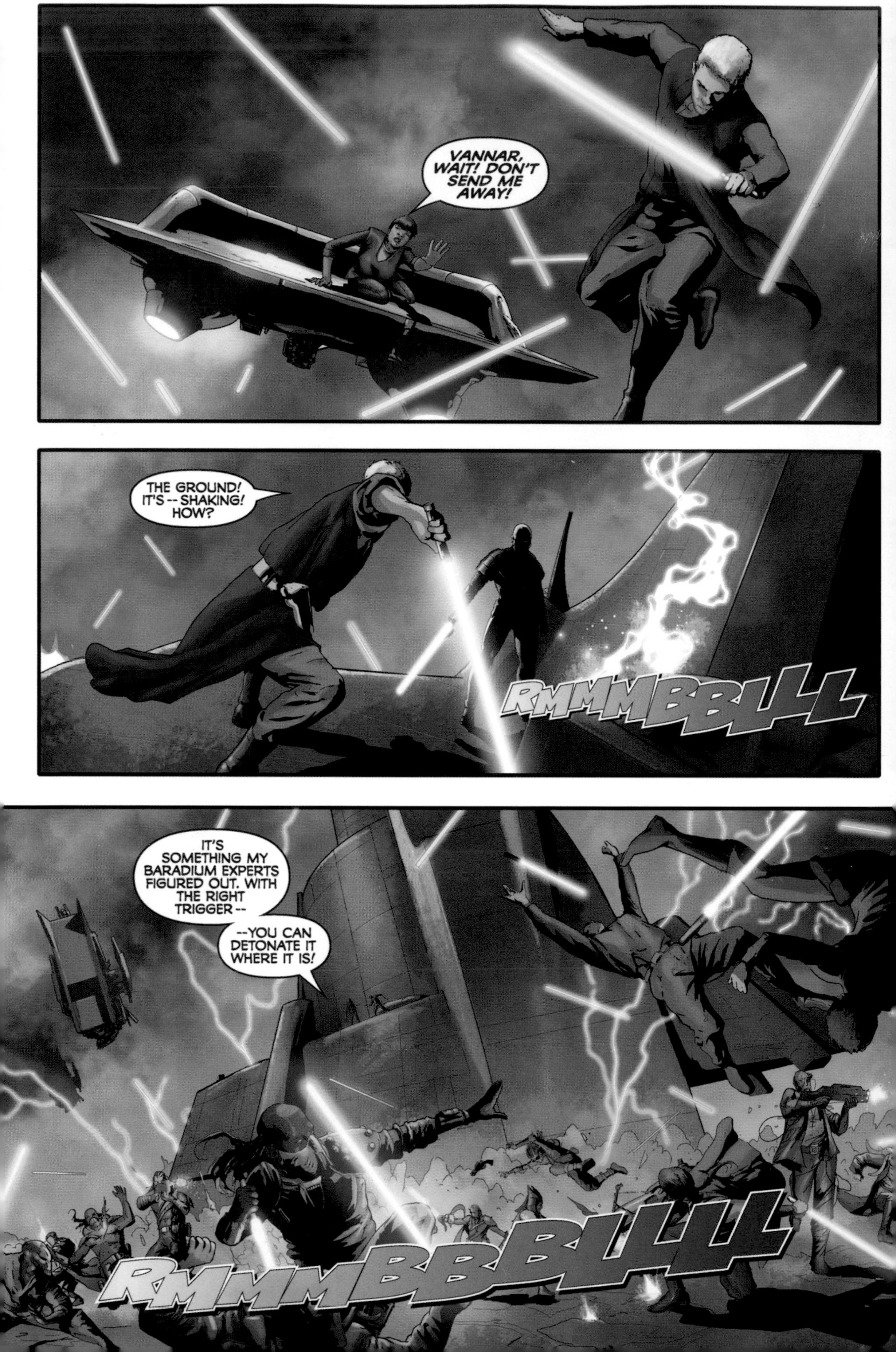
VANNAR, WAIT! DON'T SEND ME AWAY!
THE GROUND! IT'S -- SHAKING! HOW?
RMMMBBLLL
IT'S SOMETHING MY BARADIUM EXPERTS FIGURED OUT. WITH THE RIGHT TRIGGER --
--YOU CAN DETONATE IT WHERE IT IS!
RMMMBBLLL

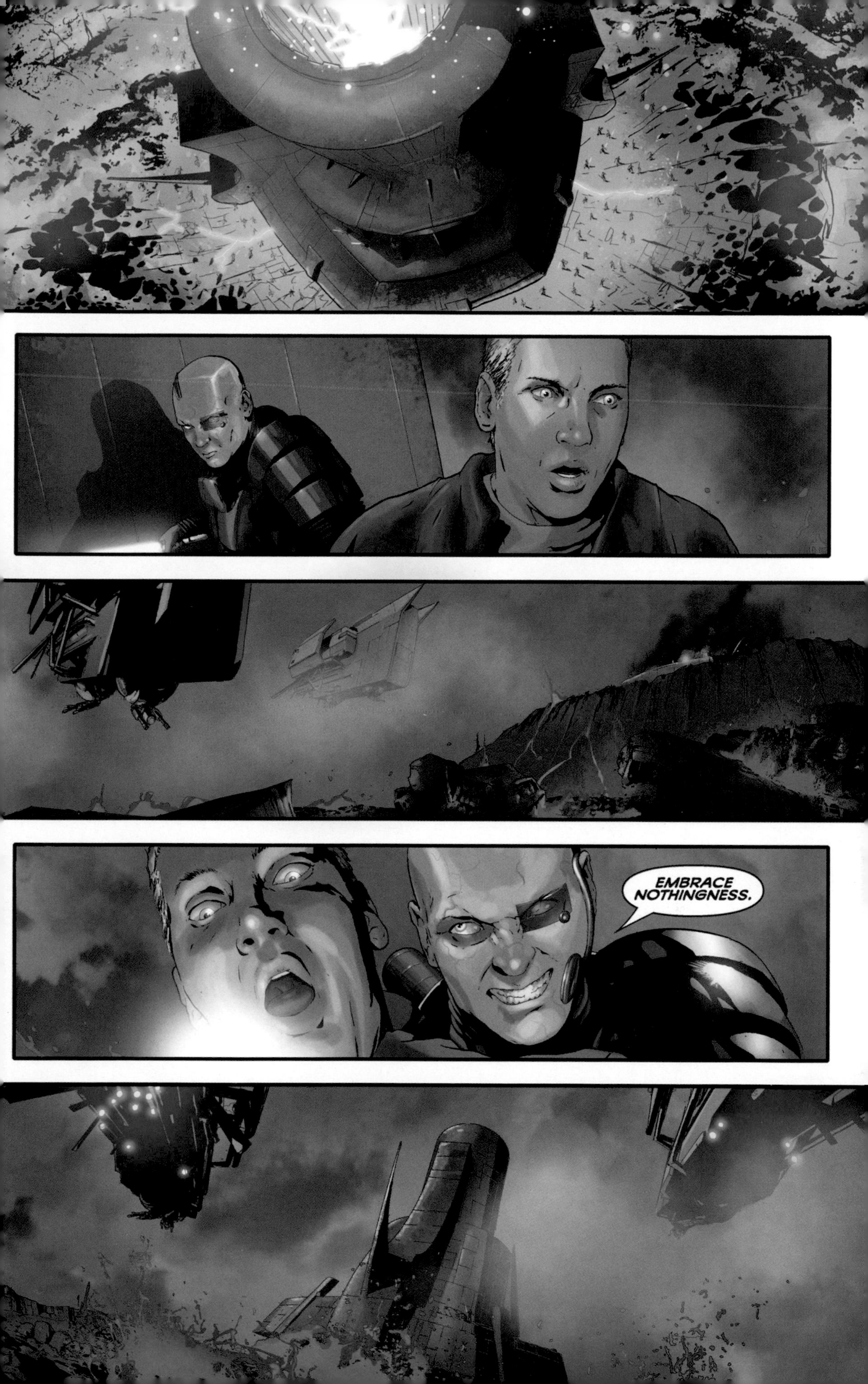
EMBRACE NOTHINGNESS.

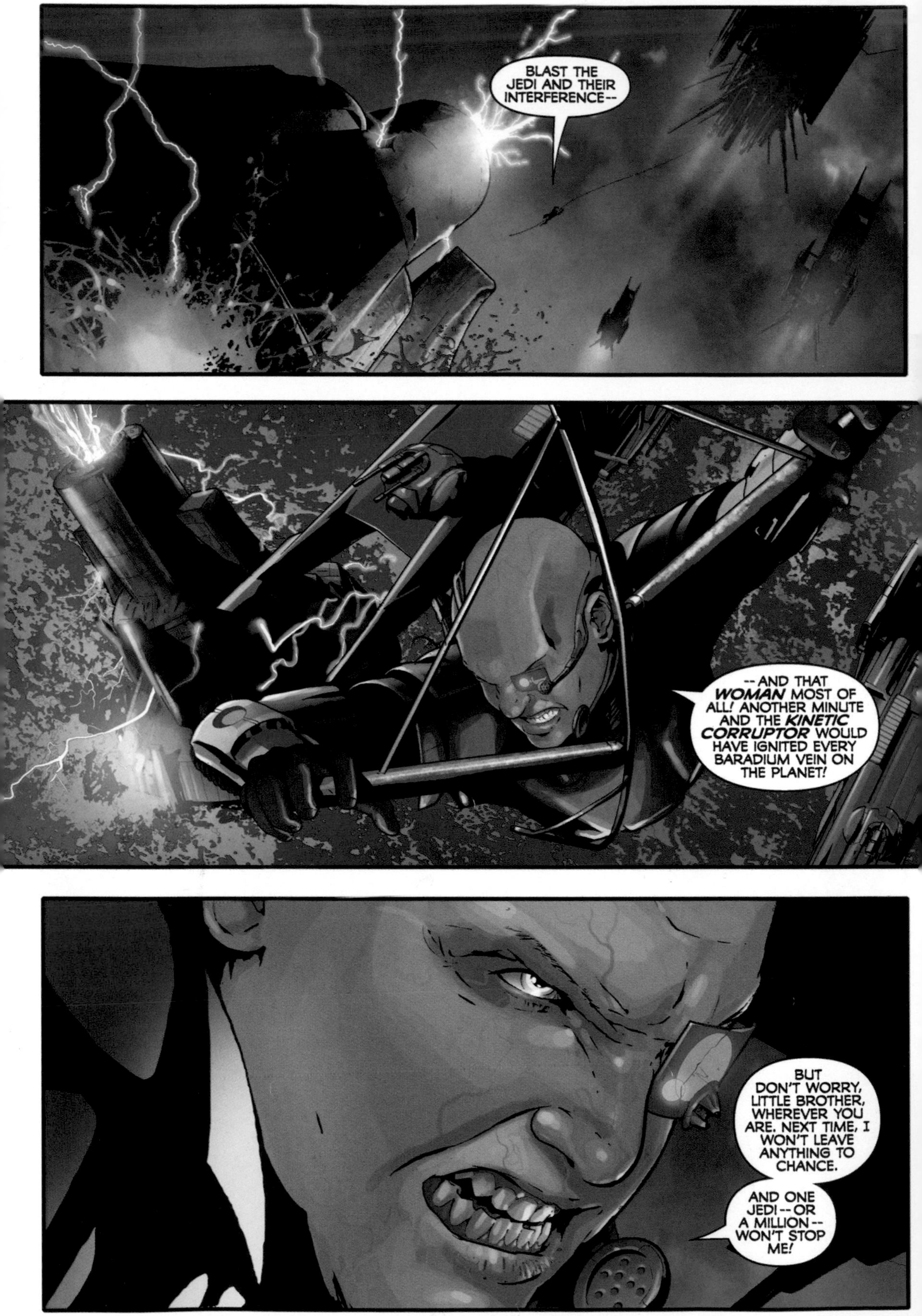
BLAST THE JEDI AND THEIR INTERFERENCE--
--AND THAT WOMAN MOST OF ALL! ANOTHER MINUTE AND THE KINETIC CORRUPTOR WOULD HAVE IGNITED EVERY BARADIUM VEIN ON THE PLANET!
BUT DON'T WORRY, LITTLE BROTHER, WHEREVER YOU ARE. NEXT TIME, I WON'T LEAVE ANYTHING TO CHANCE.
AND ONE JEDI--OR A MILLION--WON'T STOP ME!

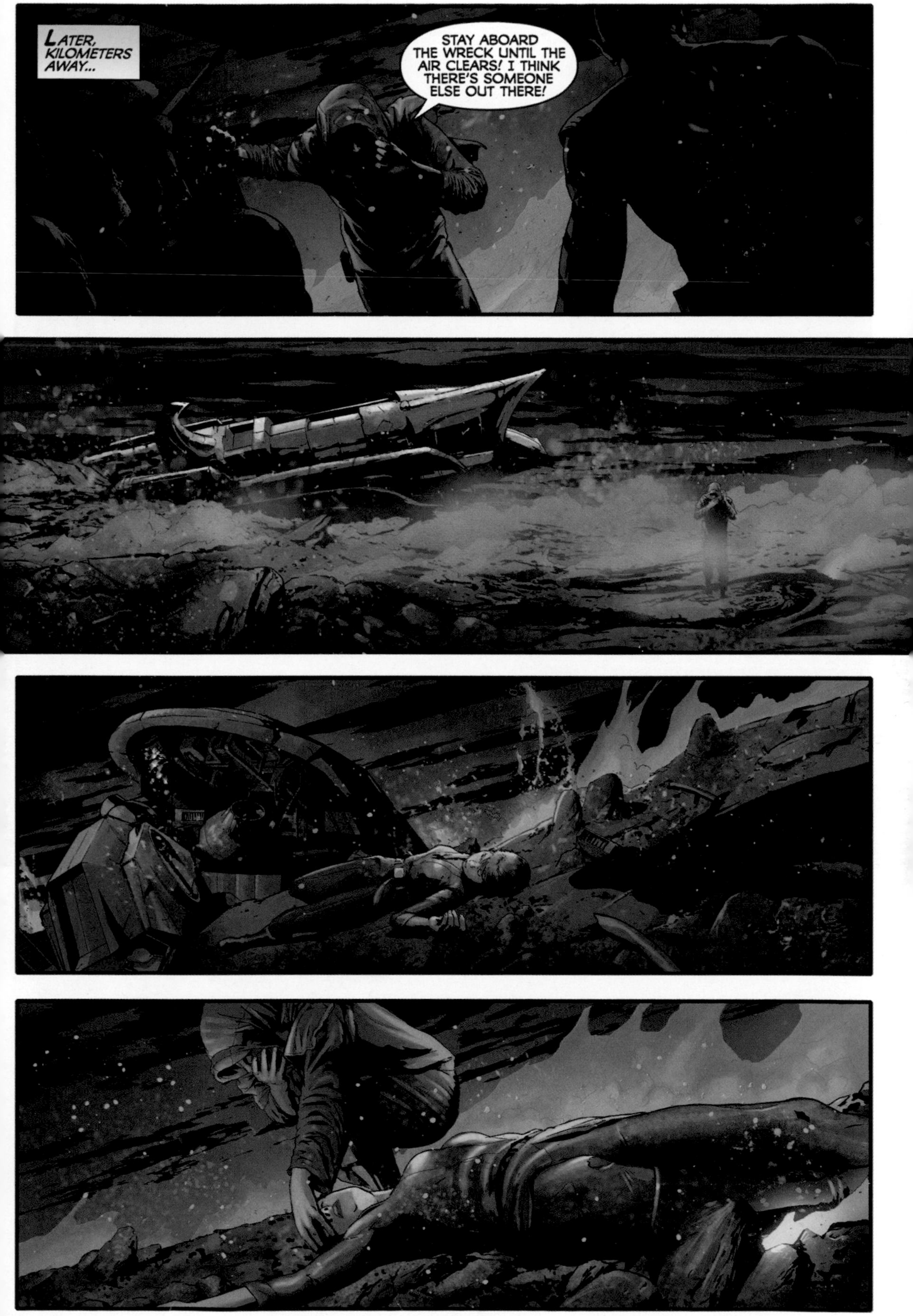
LATER, KILOMETERS AWAY...
STAY ABOARD THE WRECK UNTIL THE AIR CLEARS! I THINK THERE'S SOMEONE ELSE OUT THERE!

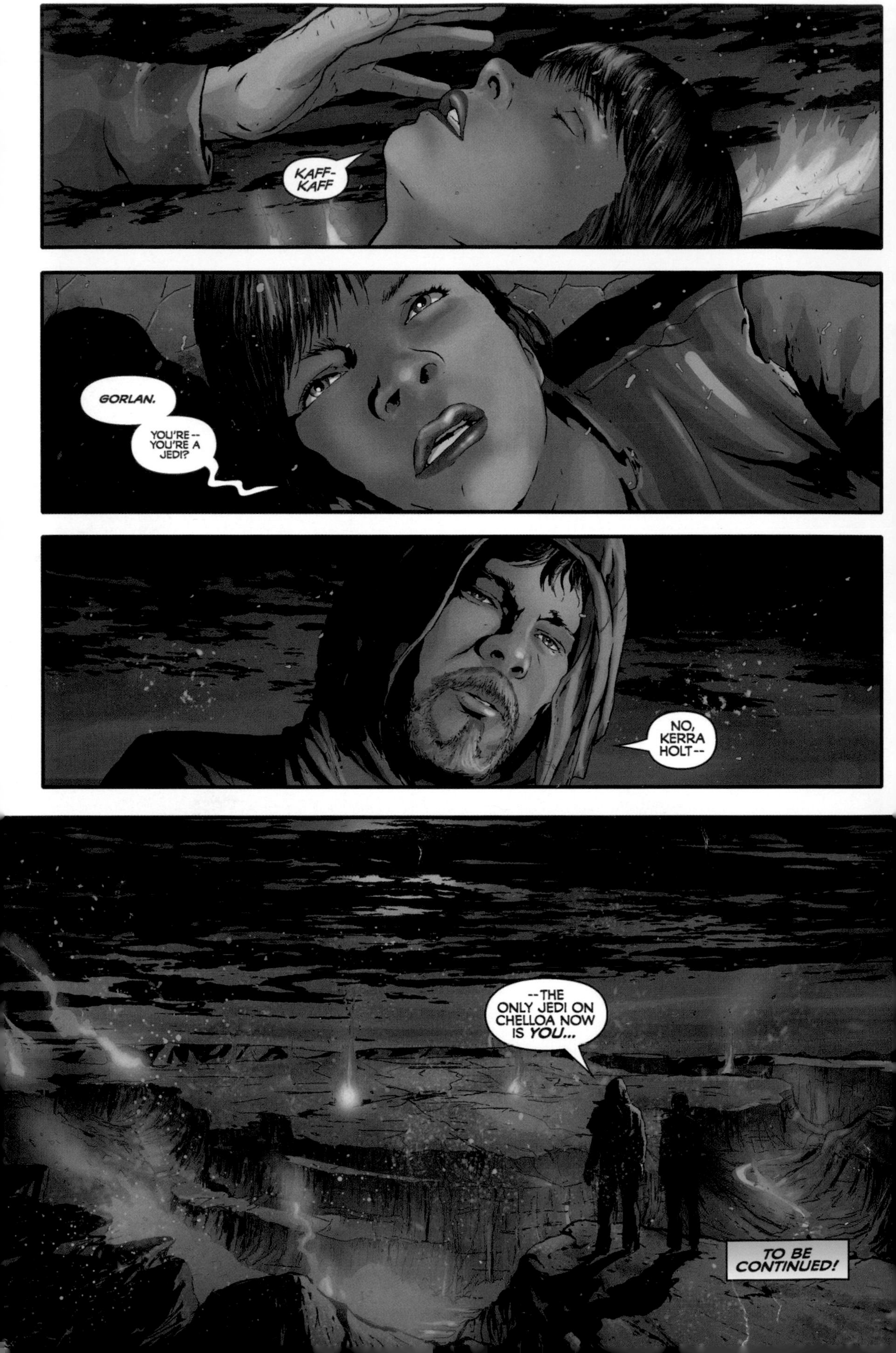
KAFF-
KAFF
GORLAN.
YOU'RE --
YOU'RE A
JEDI?
NO,
KERRA
HOLT --
-- THE
ONLY JEDI ON
CHELLOA NOW
IS *YOU*...
TO BE
CONTINUED!